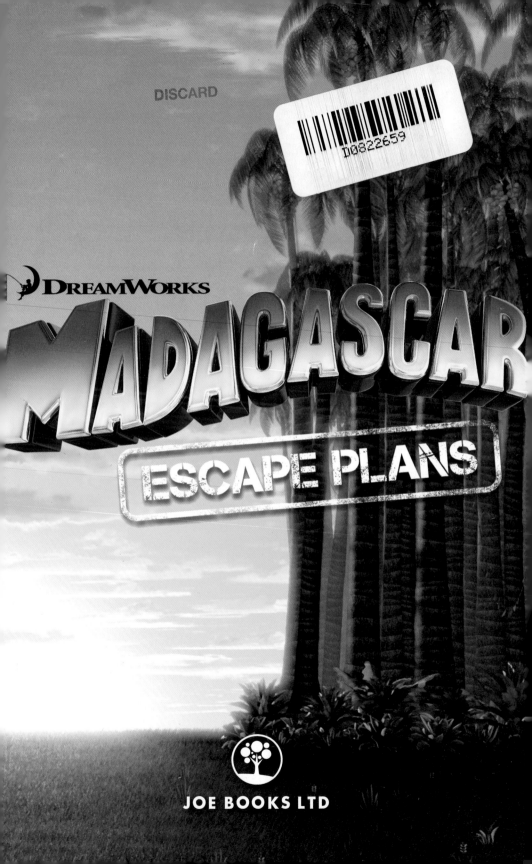

DREAMWORKS

MADAGASCAR

ESCAPE PLANS

JOE BOOKS LTD

Writers
Patrick Storck (#1, 2)
Rik Hoskin (#3, 4)

Artists
Rafael Sam (#1, #2; #4)
Benito Olea (#3)

Color Artists
Carlos Lopez (#1, 2; #4)
Juanma Aguilera (#3)

Letterer
Brandon DeStefano

Editors
Rich Young
Rachel Gluckstern

Design
Sayre Street Books

Published simultaneously in the United States and Canada by Joe Books Ltd,
489 College Street, Suite 203, Toronto, Ontario, M6G 1A5

www.joebooks.com

First Joe Books Edition: September 2017

ISBN: 978-1-772753-08-0

Library and Archives Canada Cataloguing in Publication
information is available upon request.

Printed and bound in Canada
1 3 5 7 9 10 8 6 4 2

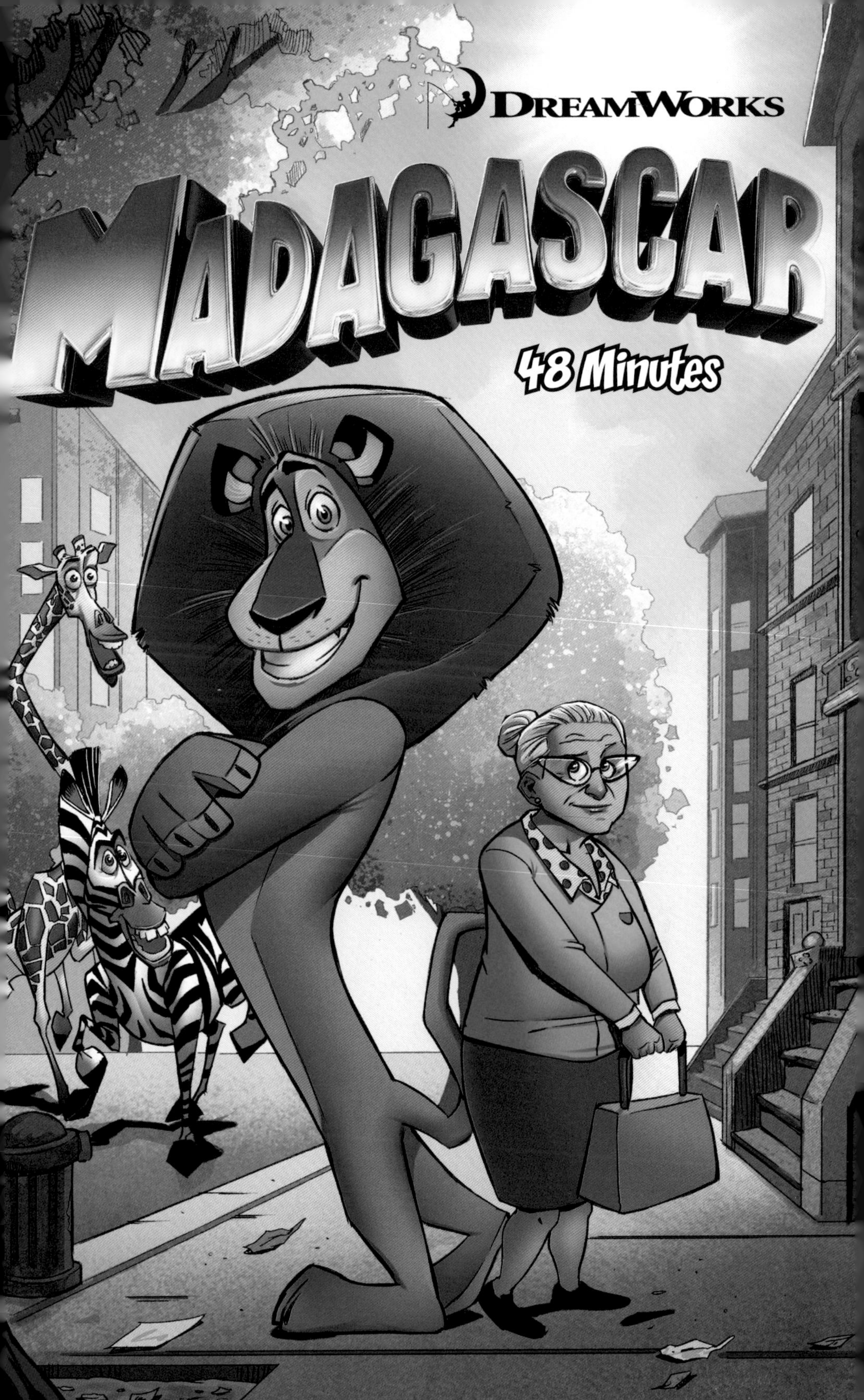
DREAMWORKS
MADAGASCAR
48 Minutes

CLAP
CLAP
CLAP
ALEX Nº 1
ALEX Nº 1

GREAT. HER AGAIN. SHE NEVER SMILES, APPLAUDS, JUST STANDS THERE SCOWLING.

SHE'S FROM A DIFFERENT GENERATION. SHE PROBABLY IS USED TO COLOSSEUM LIONS.

MORE LIKE KING OF THE BUNGLE...
YOINK!
GET BACK HERE YOU NO-GOOD PUNK!
I'VE GOT A FIVE-KNUCKLE REWARD FOR YOU IF YOU GIVE IT BACK NOW! TRUST ME, IT'S BETTER THAN WHAT ELSE I COULD OFFER!

THIS ZOO IS A NO CRIME ZONE! WHO'S GOING TO COME HERE IF THEY DON'T FEEL SAFE?

HE'S HEADING FOR THE BACK EXIT. ALEX COULD CATCH HIM!

I COULD...

FINE. I'LL GO AFTER HIM.

JUST MISSED HIM! BUT I'VE GOT THE SCENT. OLD LADY PURSE... MOTHBALLS, BUTTERSCOTCH CANDIES, AND...

FRESH STEAK...?!

WHAT THE!

O-O-V-V-E-E-R-R-K-K-I-I-L-L-L-L!!!

AS IF I DON'T HAVE ENOUGH TO DO GETTING MY PURSE BACK, NOW I'VE GOT TO DEAL WITH AN ESCAPED LION!
UNGRATEFUL OLD--
NO, I SAID I'D HELP. AND I THINK THAT STEAK WOULD BE A REASONABLE REWARD. YEAH, NO REASON TO NOT GET SOME SORT OF REWARD, RIGHT?

HEY, LADY!
YOU'RE GOING THE WRONG WAY!

HOW CAN YOU NOT SMELL THAT PURSE WITH ALL OF THOSE MOTH BALLS?

AND BRASS KNUCKLES? WHAT IS WRONG WITH YOU?

IT'S PROBABLY BETTER THIS WAY. YOU WON'T SLOW ME DOWN.

GOTTA
LOVE NEW
YORK.

IT'S ALMOST LUNCH. SO MUCH FRESH BREAD! PASTRAMI! PIZZA! SOUVLAKI!

SO MANY FOOD CARTS!
HOT DOG
HOT DOG

I MEAN, I DID TRY. BUT IF YOU LOSE THE TRAIL, YOU LOSE THE TRAIL. MAYBE I SHOULD JUST GRAB A BITE TO EAT AND HEAD BACK.

THAT DOESN'T SOUND LIKE THE KIND, HELPFUL, BIG, STRONG ALE I KNOW. BESIDES, MAYBE I YOU HELP HER, SHE MIGHT LIKE YOU MORE.
WHY DOES EVERYONE ASSUME *NEED* EVERYONE EL TO LIKE ME?

AND THE SPOTLIGHT, THE APPLAUSE, THE HOURLY SHOWS...
SOME COUNTERPOINT YOU ARE!

I'M ON YOUR SIDE! I JUST SAY PLAY INTO THE WHOLE HERO ANGLE. MAYBE YOU MAKE THE PAPERS, GET A STATUE, HAVE A LIBRARY NAMED AFTER YOU!
MY OWN LIBRARY?

ALRIGHT, TUNE OUT THE SNACK CARTS...HANG ON....PICKING UP SOMETHING AGED AND BITTER, LIKE BAD MEAT OR GOOD CHEESE...

AND TOO MUCH PERFUME...HER PURSE! THERE YOU ARE!

LOOSE KITTY! I KNOW WHAT YOU'RE AFTER!

OH GREAT...

THERE ARE TWO LAST PASSES TO THAT ALL-YOU-CAN-EAT STEAK BUFFET IN THAT PURSE, AND YOU'RE NOT GETTING THEM... *OR* THE LEFTOVERS FROM LAST NIGHT'S PASS!

ALL-YOU-CAN-EAT STEAK?!

WHY WOULD YOU NEED TWO?

ONE LITERALLY COVERS *ALL YOU CAN EAT!*

NANA

VS

ALEX

PLAYER 1

INSERT-COIN

PLAYER 2

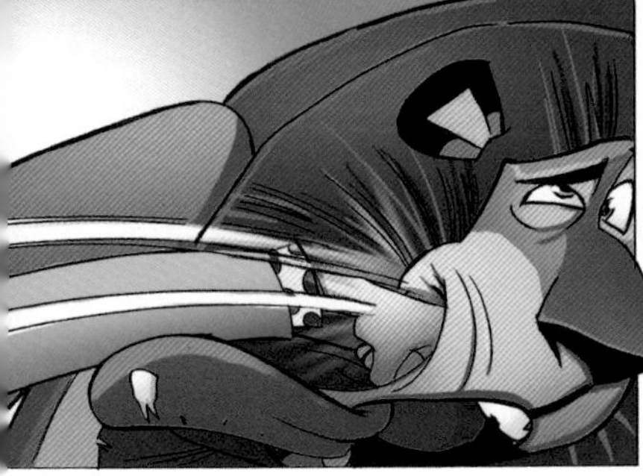

RRRAAAWWRRR!!!

CUT IT OUT

KEEN SENSE OF SMELL!

YOUR SMELLY OLD BAG, YOU SMELLY OLD BAG!

OH. YOU THINK YOU'RE A TRACKER, DO YA? WELL...FINE, ONE PASS IS BETTER THAN NONE.

DON'T THINK I'LL VOUCH FOR YOU AT THE RESTAURANT. THEY HAVE A STRICT DRESS CODE. YOU HAVE TO WEAR CLOTHES.
I CAN FIND SOMETHING. WE JUST PASSED A BIG AND TALL SHOP.
POLICE
I CAN'T UNDERSTAND YOU. ALL GROWLS! GROWL, GROWL, GROWL!
MAYBE GET A HEARING AID?
DON'T GROWL AT ME!
HOW CAN I CALL YOU THE WORST IN A PURR?
I DON'T KNOW WHAT YOU JUST SAID, BUT IT SOUNDED SARCASTIC.

GAH! A LION! ON THE LOOSE! ON THE STREET NEAR SO MANY PEOPLE! SOMEBODY HELP!
OH, FLUFFYLUMPS HERE? IT'S A STREET PERFORMANCE!
NOW! DANCE! DO YOUR STUPID LITTLE THING!
THIS IS WHY I DON'T HAVE A MANAGER.
AND ONE-TWO, ONE-TWO-THREE! JAZZ HANDS FINISH!
THANKS! FORTY CENTS! NO WONDER YOU'RE WALKING! THIS WOULDN'T PAY FOR A CAB TO THE NEXT CORNER!

GREAT. STOOL PIGEONS.
HEY! WE COULDN'T HELP BUT OVERHEAR. YOU GUYS LOOKING FOR A MISSING PURSE?
TAXI

FINE, HERE. THESE ARE LOOSE. THREE THREADS AND THAT'S IT!

OH, ***COME ON!*** YOU CAN'T EVEN TRUST FILTHY STRAY BIRDS ANY MORE!

FOLLOW US!

OH. SORRY ABOUT THE FILTHY COMMENT.

KEEP UP! WE'RE LOSING THEM!
YOU ALMOST RUINED MY SWEATER!
SLOW DOWN! DO I LOOK LIKE A GAZELLE?

MORE LIKE GAZ-ELDERLY. WHY AM I WAITING FOR YOU?

OH NO YOU DON'T! YOU'LL TAKE ALL THE STEAK FOR YOURSELF!
MAYBE I NEED IT, RUNNING AROUND FOR YOU ALL DAY, UNAPPRECIATED!

GREAT! WE LOST THEM!

BAD KITTY! WE LOST THEM!
HOW IS THIS MY FAULT?!?

AWWW, YOU TWO LOST YOUR PURSE SNATCHER?
HE'S UP THE STREET AT THE CAFÉ.
HOW DID YOU KNOW WE WERE LOOKING FOR A PURSE?
OLD LADY WITH NO PURSE? YOUNG PUNK WITH A PURSE?
EASY MATH! WE CAN TELL A RAT WHEN WE SEE ONE!

WELL, THANKS FOR RATTING HIM OUT!

IT SOUNDS MEAN WHEN YOU SAY IT.
OH, SORRY. BUT THANKS AGAIN!

NOW WHAT? THEY TELL YOU WHERE TO GET CAT CHEESE?

LET'S JUST GET YOUR STUPID PURSE SO I CAN GET SOME STEAK AND GO HOME.

Ninja Coffee
Heroes Coffee
Medieval Coffee
Centural Coffee
Coffee

Mocca Chinos

We Care a Latte

Captain Cookie

Turn And Coffee

WELL THIS IS HOPELESS.
WE'VE ONLY BEEN ONE BLOCK. HOW MUCH COFFEE DO PEOPLE NEED?

HEY! BUDDY! CAN I TALK TO YOU, GATO Y GATO?
WHATEVER. SURE. I GUESS. WHAT?
WE'RE TRYING TO FIND A THIEF.
SO? SCRATCH ME. DON'T. ARE WE FRIENDS? I DON'T CARE.
THE RATS AND THE PIGEONS WERE NO HELP.
BIG SURPRISE. I DON'T LIKE THEM. THEY DON'T LIKE ME. DO THEY? WHAT DID THEY SAY?
CAN YOU JUST HELP US? MAYBE GET THE WORD OUT?
SURE. I MEAN WHEN I GET AROUND TO IT. I'M BUSY.
OKAY. WHAT DO YOU NEED?
A PURSE THAT SMELLS LIKE HER.
SHE SMELLS LIKE DOGS. DOG LADIES DON'T FEED CATS.
SHE PROMISED TO FEED ME!
THAT'S YOU. WHAT'S IN IT FOR ME?

MROW

MROW

MROW

MROW

MROW
HOT DOG
HOT DOG

SNIFF! GAHH! CHOO! I GIVE IN! WHEEZE! GO AWAY! ***HELP!!!***

LOOKS LIKE THEY ARRESTED HIM ON... JUST CLAWS.

POLICE

NUNCHAKUS...

GRANOLA...

GRENADE...

I GUESS I OWE YOU A STEAK DINNER.

AND I'VE DEFINITELY WORKED UP AN APPETITE. I MIGHT EVEN HAVE THE SALAD! JUST KIDDING. WHY EVEN HAVE SALAD IN THE SAME BUILDING AS ALL-YOU-CAN-EAT STEAK?

I'M SORRY, BUT THE MANAGEMENT REFUSES TO LET IN A LION, UNLESS HE'S A SEEING EYE LION. STRICT POLICY, SORRY.

MAYBE I'M BLIND, PIERRE!
THEN HOW DID YOU JUST READ MY NAME TAG?

SORRY, I TRIED. LOOKS LIKE YOU'RE ON YOUR OWN.

SHOULD'VE EXPECTED THIS. THANKS ANYWAY...

IF YOU EVER DO GET INTO A BUFFET, GET A VINYL PURSE. IT'S AMAZING HOW MUCH EXTRA FOOD YOU CAN GET INTO ONE OF THESE!
YOU'RE A GENIUS! AN EVIL GENIUS, STILL PRETTY SURE ABOUT THAT...
THIS MAKES US EVEN. FOR NOW...
THE END.

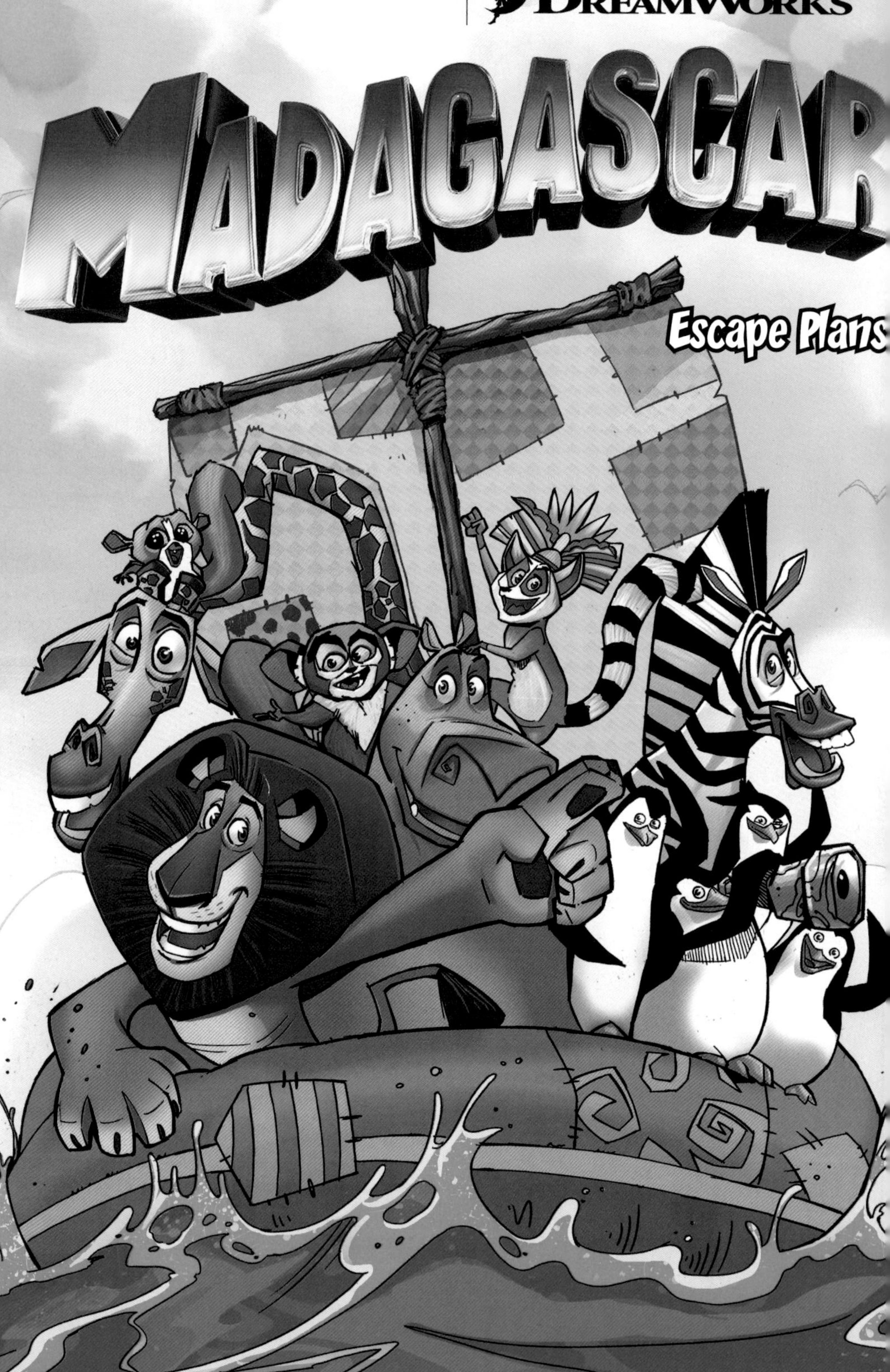
DreamWorks
MADAGASCAR
Escape Plans

WE HAVE GOT IT *PRETTY* GOOD HERE!

SUN, SURF, SLACKING!

NOTHING BUT A NICE COOL BREEZE TO PASS ALONG THE DAY!

NO GERMS, NO STRESS, NOT A CARE IN THE WORLD!

THE HUSTLE AND BUSTLE! PEOPLE ALWAYS HAVING TO BE SOMEWHERE TO DO SOMETHING, SEE SOME SHOW, LUNCH AT WHATEVER HOT NEW PLACE...

THE PEOPLE, THE KIDS...

THE AUDIENCES, THE REGULAR FEEDING SCHEDULE...ICE CREAM...

YEP, WE'RE HOME-SICK. AND YOU KNOW HOW I HATE BEEN ANY KIND OF SICK.

WE'RE TRAPPED! WE'RE LOST AT SEA!

CALM DOWN. THERE'S NO NEED TO PANIC. ALEX, TALK SOME SENSE INTO THEM.

WE NEED TO GET OUT OF HERE!!!

A JOURNEY THROUGH DEATH-DEFYING THINGS OUT OF NOWHERE, AND MAYBE A ROMANTIC SUBPLOT, NOT NAMING NAMES, AND THEN THERE'S A BIG LESSON OR MAYBE SOMETHING WE FEEL IN THE RIGHT HERE. GETS ME EVERY TIME.

JULIEN Nº 1

WE SHALL USE ALL OF THE OUNCES OR MILLILITERS OF OUR WISDOM IN ESCAPE, AS EVIDENC BY ALL OF THE LEMURS YOU DON'T SEE RIGHT NOW, WHO HAD TO HAVE GONE SOMEWHERE. SEE HOW GOOD THEY ARE?

SO HOW MANY BOATS HAVE YOU MADE?
THIS IS A RAFT!
OKAY, HOW MANY RAFTS HAVE YOU MADE?
OH, I'M ONLY HELPING WITH PART OF IT!
YOU'RE NOT GOING TO GIVE ME AN ANSWER, ARE YOU?
IT IS FORBIDDEN!
I'M JUST SAYING, IF WE PAINT EVERY OTHER BAMBOO POLE, THEN NAMING IT THE S.S. MARTY IS A NO-BRAINER!
NONE OF THIS LOOKS STURDY. AT ALL.
YET!

I KNOW THEY ASKED FOR A TIKI ROOM, BUT I REALLY DON'T THINK TORCHES ON A WOODEN BOAT IS A GOOD IDEA!

IT WORKED FOR THE VIKINGS! THEY BURNED BOATS ALL THE TIME!

NO, THEY DIDN'T! THEY ONLY DID THAT WHEN--NEVER MIND. JUST NO TORCHES.

CAREFUL! LIFT WITH YOUR KNEES!
BUT OUR HANDS HAVE MORE FINGERS!

WHICH WAY ARE WE TAKING THESE?

I WAS TOLD UP THE BEACH!

I HEARD BACK TO CAMP!

I'VE SEEN THIS BIT...
NOOOOOO THANK YOU.

FELLA, THAT'S ONE HECK OF A SWIM. BEST OPTION IS WE DIG OUR WAY TO FREEDOM!
AS LONG AS WE STAY IN THE SWEET SPOT BETWEEN MURKY SEA AND MOLTEN LAVA, WE SHOULD BE GOOD.

WHY DON'T WE JUST BUILD A RAFT LIKE THEY'RE DOING?

TEAMWORK? THAT'S JUST WHAT THEY'D BE EXPECTING!
IT WOULD MEAN THEY DO HALF THE WORK AS WELL, THOUGH.

BUT LOOK AT THEM! UNORGANIZED, UNSKILLED, THEIR ENTIRE OPERATION IS A COMPLETE MESS!
IT DOESN'T HAVE TO BE. I BET WE COULD GET THOSE TROOPS IN SHAPE IN NO TIME!

I WON'T SAY YOU'RE RIGHT, BUT I CAN'T SAY YOU'RE WRONG...

GOOD CALL, RINGTAIL, BRINGING IN OUR EXTRACTION AND CONSTRUCTION EXPERTISE!
I WHAT? OH, THAT DOES SOUND LIKE ME, IF IT WAS A GOOD DECISION.

PINSTRIPE FELLA-- LESS ROPE, MORE GLUE! ZIPPY! OTHER WAY AROUND! RICO, CON-STRUCTION! PINCH THAT FUSE!

I LOVE IT WHEN A PLAN COMES TOGETHER!

A PLAN? OH, YOU DO THINK OF EVERYTHING!

IT HAS A TIKI LOUNGE, A COMEDY CLUB, A NICE DECK WITH POOL FLOATIES (THE OCEAN IS YOUR POOL NOW), SHUFFLEBOARD, A GYM TO WORK OUT...

HOMEWARD BOUND!
THIS IS GOING TO BE A FANTASTIC VOYAGE!

A REAL SEA QUEST!
AS LONG AS WE DON'T WIND UP 20,000 LEAGUES UNDER IT!

WE SHOULD STILL BE GOING FORWARD, RIGHT? MAYBE THE WAVES ARE AN OPTICAL ILLUSION.

LIKE WHEN I DO THIS--

IT'S JUST CALM. MAYBE WHEN THE WIND PICKS UP WE CAN--

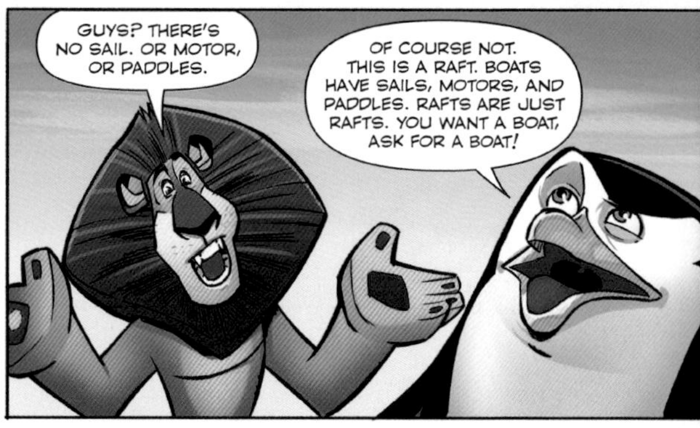
GUYS? THERE'S NO SAIL. OR MOTOR, OR PADDLES.
OF COURSE NOT. THIS IS A RAFT. BOATS HAVE SAILS, MOTORS, AND PADDLES. RAFTS ARE JUST RAFTS. YOU WANT A BOAT, ASK FOR A BOAT!

HOW'D SHE GET SO FAST?
HIPPOS ARE DESCENDED FROM WHALES!
AMAZINGLY, THAT'S TRUE.

I'M CATCHING MY FIRST TUBE TODAY, SIR!

WE SAW YOU ALL SWIMMING BACK, AND FIGURED WE WOULD GET STARTED ON A DO-OVER.

WE HEARD SOMEONE SAY "SOMETHING SOME-THING *YOU BOAT*," AND THOUGHT--
SUBMARINE!

IT'S VERY NICE, AS I DO SAY SO MYSELF.

DOESN'T BAMBOO FLOAT?
WE LOADED THE BOTTOM WITH ROCKS SO YOU SHOULD BE FINE.
GULP!

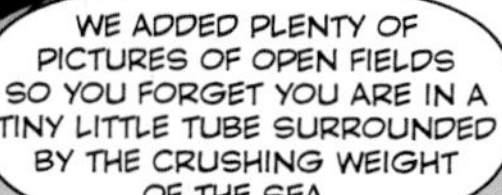

WE ADDED PLENTY OF PICTURES OF OPEN FIELDS SO YOU FORGET YOU ARE IN A TINY LITTLE TUBE SURROUNDED BY THE CRUSHING WEIGHT OF THE SEA.

GULP!

AND WE DESIGNED IT AFTER THOSE SHARK CAGES SO WHEN, I MEAN IF, A SCHOOL OF SHARKS ATTACKS YOU SHOULD BE FINE!
SHOULD BE?
GUUULLLPPP!!!

HERE GOES NOTHING!

YOU MEAN OUR CHANCES OF SURVIVAL?

DOWN

WELL AT LEAST THE CONTROLS ARE EASY.

HEY, MELMAN! NOW I KNOW HOW YOU SEE THE WORLD!

SHOULDN'T ALL OF THE WATER BE OUT THERE?

SEALS WOULD JUST ATTRACT MORE SHARKS!
THEY DIDN'T GIVE US A GOOD SEAL!

QUICK! SOMEBODY HIT THE UP BUTTON!

NO CAN DO! THIS SUB HAS NO UP BUTTON.

WE NEED TO DROP SOME ROCKS!

I THINK I JUST DID.

ON IT!

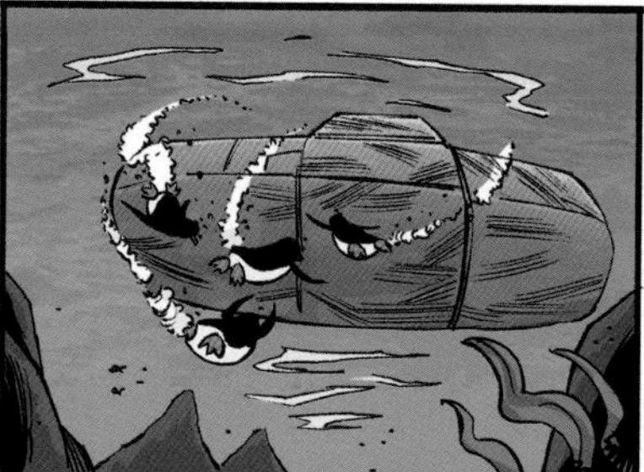

WHAT WAS THAT?!?
DAVY JONES COMING TO SAY HI?

NOPE!

WOULD WE GO ONE AT A TIME?
HOW WOULD YOU AIM IT?
THE AIR FORCE, EH?

I DON'T WANT TO BE AN ANGEL, BLUE OR OTHERWISE...
NOPE, NO WAY. NOT A CHANCE!

DON'T WORRY! WE'LL TEST IT ON MORT?
YAYYYY!

WHAT?

WHERE IS THE SEAT BELT?
GOES AGAINST THE WHOLE POINT. YOU'LL SEE IN A SECOND.
HERE'S YOUR IN-FLIGHT SNACK.
BUT I'M ALLERGIC TO--
I REGRET NOTHING!!!!
CAN SOMEONE GO FIND HIM?
JUST WHEN YOU THOUGHT YOU UNDERSTOOD PHYSICS...

HERE'S AN IDEA--WE DRIVE BACK!
KEYS!
COUGH
JUST MAKE SURE TO KEEP THE WINDOWS UP FOR THE FIRST FEW HUNDRED MILES.
AND EVERYONE MAKE SURE YOU THOUGHT OF EVERYTHING BEFORE WE LEAVE. WE DON'T WANT TO HAVE TO TURN BACK.
I DON'T THINK THIS IS A GOOD IDEA WE'RE FROM NEW YOR WE NEVER GOT OUR DRIVER'S LICENSES.

REMEMBER, THIS IS A SUPPLY RUN ONLY. JUST THE ESSENTIALS. ROPE, FUEL, FOOD, THIS PRETTY SHELL!

LOOK AT YOU, LITTLE GUY! SOME CLAM JUST UP AND LEFT YOU HERE? WHAT A WASTE!

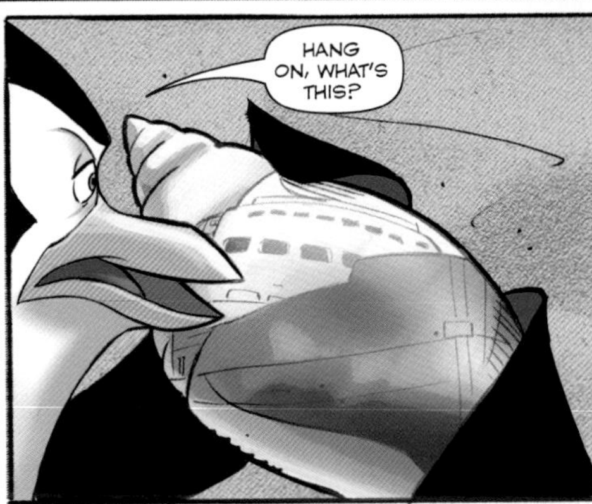
HANG ON, WHAT'S THIS?

I'M A LITTLE SURPRISED WE FORGOT ABOUT THIS.
I DIDN'T! BEEN CHECKING ON HER EACH DAWN, MAKING SURE SHE'S GASSED UP AND READY TO GO!

AND HOW IS THE FUEL SITUATION?
TOTALLY EMPTY, SIR. SAME AS BEFORE.
GOOD! I LOVE A CHALLENGE.

NOPE...
THAT ONE DIDN'T
WORK...SUNK...BURNED...
SUNK...IMPLODED...
I'M BLACK AND WHITE, AND I'VE READ THESE ALL OVER. WE'VE TRIED EVERYTHING!
NOT EVERYTHING! WHAT DO YOU KNOW ABOUT WORMHOLE THEORY?
THAT'S THEORETICAL QUANTUM PHYSICS. WE CAN'T EVEN BUILD A BOAT.
FANDOM QUIZZICKS? YOU TALK NONSENSE. NO! WE TUNNEL YOU BACK LIKE AN EARTHWORM THROUGH A LITTLE HOLE. HOW HARD CAN IT BE?

SORRY, GUYS.
FACE IT. WE'RE STUCK HERE.
AT LEAST ON LAND WE WON'T DROWN.
IT'S REALLY NOT SO BAD HERE. WE'RE WITH OUR FRIENDS, EACH OTHER, RIGHT?

PLUS THERE IS THE FOOD, THE PARTIES, GAME NIGHT, YOU LOOK LIKE YOU WOULD ENJOY CANASTA...

AND IF YOU WANT TO HANG OUT IN THE PLANE, WE THROW SOME SWEET MAMA PAJAMA JAMMIE JAMS. WE FIRE UP THE ENGINES, GET THE LIGHTS GOING, SOME COOL TUNES--

THE PLANE WORKS?!?

SURE, PROBABLY, BUT YOU SEEMED SO SET ON THE BOAT IDEA. I GUESS WE COULD TRY FLYING IT TOO. WANT TO GIVE IT A SHOT?

YES!!!
WHAT HAPPENS NEXT? YOU'VE ALREADY SEEN IT IN *MADAGASCAR: ESCAPE 2 AFRICA!*

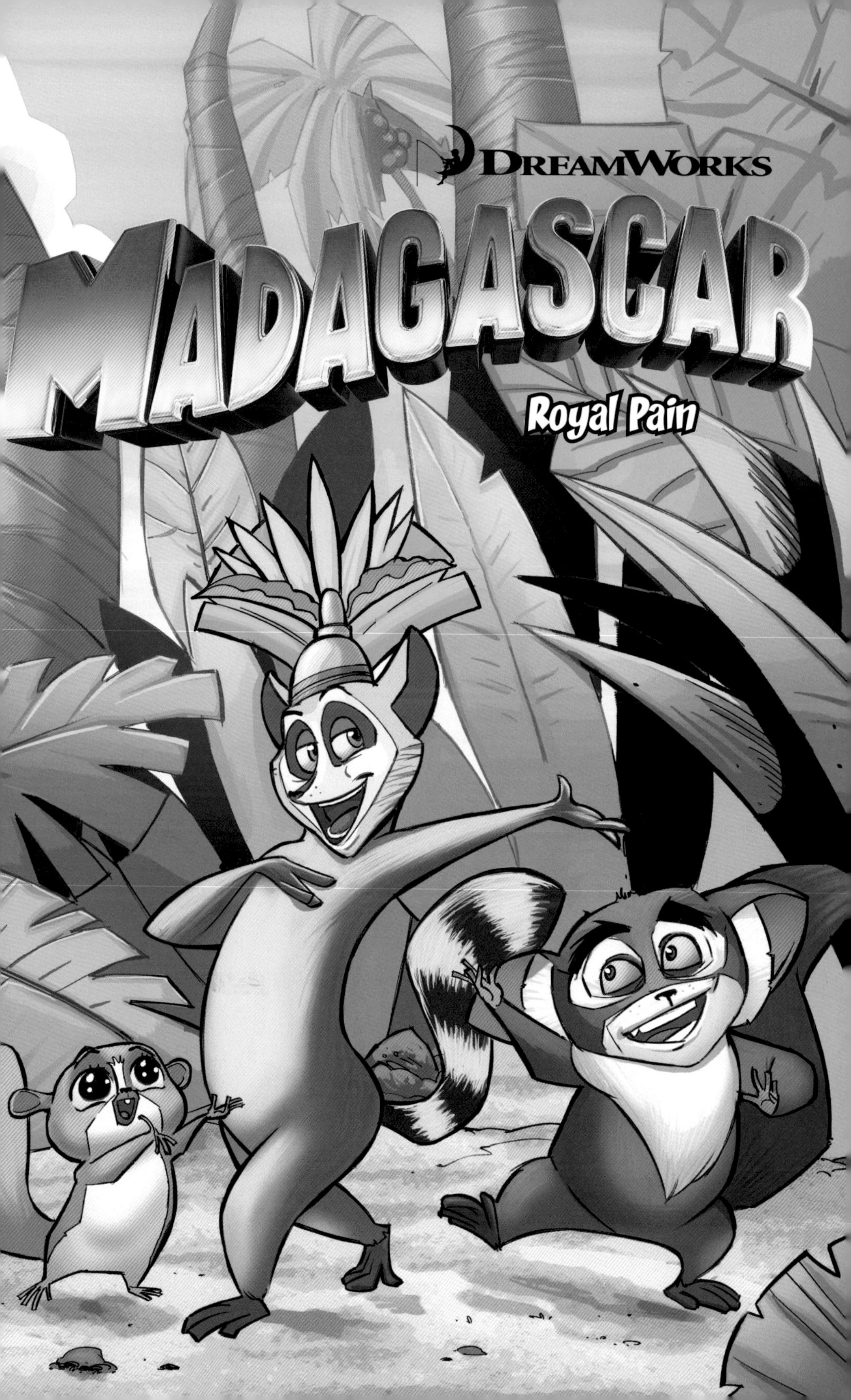
DreamWorks
MADAGASCAR
Royal Pain

MADAGASCAR!
DID YOU MISS ME?

I BET YOU *DID!* HOW COULD ANYONE *NOT* MISS ME? I'M UTTERLY *ADORABLE!*

I KNOW I'VE *MISSED* YOU!

MWAH MWAH

...BUT HE WILL!
IT'S SO GOOD TO BE BACK! I'D LIKE TO THANK YOU ALL FOR COMING OUT TO GREET ME!
IT MEANS--
HEY! WHERE IS EVERYONE?
MAURICE? WHERE IS MY MAGNIFICENT "WELCOME HOME" PARTY?
TOLD YOU!

SHORTLY...
I'M SURE THE PARTY'S HERE SOMEWHERE, YOUR HIGHNESS.
MAYBE IT'S A SURPRISE PARTY!
BOO! SURPRISE! HEE-HEE-HEE! I SCARED ME!

OF COURSE, A SURPRISE PARTY! MORT, YOU ARE A GENIUS!
A SLOW-WITTED, IRRITATING, AND DECIDEDLY UNDERWHELMING KIND OF A GENIUS, BUT A GENIUS ALL THE SAME.

NOW, IF I WAS A SURPRISE PARTY FOR THE GREATEST KING OF ALL TIME, WHERE WOULD I HIDE?
MORT, WHAT ARE YOU DOING?
I GOT FRIGHTENED! MY IMAGINARY SURPRISE PARTY WAS TOO SCARY!
SIGH

SHHHH! I HEAR SOMETHING! IT MUST BE...

...MY PARTY!
FUNKY MUSIC!
PRETTY DANCERS!
THOSE THINGS...WHATEVER THEY'RE CALLED!
AH-HUM! MAY I HELP YOU?
OH, YOU JUST POPPED UP LIKE A CK-IN-THE-BOX MAN. ELL ME, JACK-IN-THE-BOX MAN, AM I LATE FOR MY PARTY?
NO, WAIT, THAT'S IMPOSSIBLE. IT'S MY PARTY, HOW COULD I--
AH-HUM!
THIS PARTY IS MY PARTY. IT'S HELD BY ME, FOR MY SUBJECTS. AND YOU--
--DON'T--
--BELONG!
YOUR SUBJECTS? BUT I AM THEIR RULER--

Gasp
Gasp
--KING JULIEN!
Gasp
Gasp

UM, YOUR MAJESTY-- EVERYONE'S STARING.
SO I NOTICED--IT MUST BE THAT THEY HAVE MISSED ME.

MISSED YOU?!!! YOU'VE BEEN GONE FOR SO LONG WE HOPED YOU HAD LEFT FOREVER!
AS YOUR SUCCESSOR, I, PRINCE AUGUSTINE, HAVE BEEN PERFORMING ALL ROYAL DUTIES IN YOUR ABSENCE--

--INCLUDING EATING GOOD FOOD, HOLDING PLANNING MEETINGS, OVERSEEING PARTIES, PARTYING WITH OVERSEERS, EATING MORE FOOD, BOSSING LEMURS ABOUT, MAKING UP SILLY LAWS, RETRACTING SAID LAWS WHEN IT WAS OBVIOUS THAT THEY WERE DANGEROUS, ETCETERA, ETCETERA.
SOUNDS LIKE HE'S DONE A THOROUGH JOB, YOUR HIGHNESS.

THESE ANIMALS DON'T NEED YOU BACK. THEY DON'T WANT YOU BACK. I THINK IT'S TIME YOU ABDICATE-- GIVE ME YOUR CROWN!
GIVE YOU MY CROWN? NEVER! IT MATCHES ALL MY MOODS!
WELL, WE CANNOT HAVE TWO RULERS!

THEN WHAT WOULD YOU SUGGEST?
A CONTEST! ME AGAINST YOU TO PROVE WHO HA THE SUPERIOR ROY CREDENTIALS!
TO THE WINNER GOES THE CROWN, WHILE THE LOSER MU LEAVE MADAGASCA FOREVER!
AGREED!
YOU DON'T STAND A SNOW-BALL'S CHANCE IN A PLACE WHERE IT SNOWS INFREQUENTLY, MISTER PRINCE! WITH THE HELP OF MY DEVOTED SUBJECTS, I SHALL...
UM-- SIRE?

WHAT IS IT, MAURICE? YOU ARE INTERRUPTING SOME QUITE EXCEPTIONAL SMACK TALK HERE!
YOUR "DEVOTED SUBJECTS" APPEAR TO BE FOLLOWING PRINCE AUGUSTINE.
HMMM, YOU'RE RIGHT. THEN I SUPPOSE IT'S JUST YOU, ME, AND...
...WHERE IS MORT?
HE'S

DAY 1
CHALLENGE 1: A ROYAL BALL
I WOULD LIKE TO WELCOME YOU ON BEHALF OF PRINCE AUGUSTINE!
JUDGE
JUDGE
JUDGE
ARE WE READY YET, MAURICE? THE SILLY NATIVES ARE GETTING RESTLESS!
I'M WORKING AS FAST AS I CAN, YOUR ROYALNESS. MORT AND I SPENT ALL AFTERNOON CONSTRUCTING YOUR PALACE!
INDEED, LOOK AT YOU--YOU'RE SWEATING!
THAT'S NOT SWEAT, IT'S DRIPS. YOUR ICE SCULPTURES AREN'T GOING TO LAST LONG IN THIS HEAT.
NONSENSE! NOW, LET'S WELCOME OUR--

--HONORED GUESTS...?!
SLIP
totter

CRASH
totter

CREEEK
CRASH

CREEEK
CRASH

WELL, HOW DO YOU RATE MY ROYAL BALL?
0
ISN'T IT MAGNIFICENT?!
PRINCE AUGUSTINE - 1
KING JULIEN - 0

DAY 2

THE AUGUSTINE

THE KING JULIEN

I NAME THIS SHIP THE AUGUSTINE!
MAY ALL WHO SAIL IN HER HAVE A JOLLY SPLENDID TIME!
HE'S SO HANDSOME!
MY HERO!
CRASH
HOORAY
HELLO, EVERYONE--
GET ON WITH IT!
--YES, SOME-ONE DOWN THERE CAN'T WAIT TO BE SEASICK!
I NAME THIS SHIP...
YOU STINK!
PSST! WHERE IS THE BOTTLE? THE BOTTLE TO BREAK ON THE SHIP?
MAURICE, WE MUST FIND A BOTTLE OF CHAMPAGNE WITH WHICH TO LAUNCH THIS SHIP!
?
ERRR, THERE WAS THAT CRATE THAT WASHED UP CLOSE TO--
I DO NOT NEED THE BOTTLE'S LIFE STORY, MAURICE! LET'S GO!
ROYAL TECHNICAL HITCH, BACK IN A MOMENT, EVERYONE!
MORT, COVER FOR US!
UM...?

SO...
MAURICE? HAVE YOU FOUND MY *CHAMPAGNE* YET?
YES, SIRE, BUT I CAN'T *DECIDE* BETWEEN THE *BOLLINGER* OR THE *BRUT 2005!*
MAURICE?
YES, YOUR MAJESTY?
THUMP THUMP THUMP
IT'S BEEN AN HOUR ALREADY! JUST CHOOSE ONE! THE SHIP'S NOT GOING TO DRINK IT!!!
EVENTUALLY...
I AM PROUD TO NAME THIS SHIP *THE KING JULIEN*.
THE KING JULIEN
MAY ALL WHO SAIL IN HER...
...GO *PLA-A-A-ACES!*
HOW DID I DO?
0
0
0
PRINCE AUGUSTINE -
KING JULIEN - 0

AY 3

CHALLENGE 3:
THE CHARITY EVENT

I BELIEVE THAT A ***RULER*** IS ONLY AS GOOD AS THE ***SUBJECTS*** HE RULES!

THAT IS WHY, TODAY, I AM OPENING THIS ***CRÈCHE*** FOR THE ***YOUNGEST*** WITHIN OUR FINE COMMUNITY!

I'VE NEVER ***HEARD*** OF SUCH A THING, MAURICE! RULERS DON'T ***WORRY*** ABOUT THEIR SUBJECTS, THEY'RE ***TOO BUSY RULING!***

PHILANTHROPY IS ALL THE RAGE THIS SEASON, YOUR MAJESTICNESS.

AND IT'LL NO DOUBT ***SCORE POINTS*** WITH THE COMPETITION JUDGES.

...AND SO, IT GIVES ME ***GREAT PLEASURE*** TO OPEN THIS ***FACILITY*** FOR ALL OF YOU, MY ***FABULOUS*** SUBJECTS!

IT'S SO ***SICKENING***, MAURICE! WHAT CAN WE DO THAT WOULD BE--

SHORTLY...
NEVER LET IT BE SAID THAT JUST BECAUSE I, KING JULIEN, AM BETTER THAN YOU--
--THAT I DO NOT WANT YOU TO GET BETTER!
WHICH IS WHY I HAVE BUILT THIS, THE KING JULIEN WELLNESS CENTER, A PLACE FOR THOSE IRRITATING NUISANCES AMONG YOU WHO SUFFER--
SNIFF SNIFF
--WITH YOUR COMMON COUGHS AND SICKENING SPLUTTERS, YOUR DISGUSTING COLDS AND FILTHY VIRUSES--
--ALL THOSE TERRIBLE DISEASES THAT COULD CREEP UP ON YOU AT ANY MOMENT--
SNIIIIFF
LET ME OUT OF HERE!
aachOOOo

GET THEM OFF ME! GET THE GERMS OFF ME!!!

WAS IT *SOMETHING* I SAID?

UM... ERRR...

DAY 4
CHALLENGE 4: THE SPORT OF KINGS
ALL SET FOR TODAY'S *RACE*, YOUR MAJESTY?
OF COURSE, MAURICE. I LOVE TO RACE! THE WIND IN MY FUR, THE ROAR OF THE CROWDS.
NOW, REMIND ME *WHAT IT IS* THAT WE ARE *RACING*!
HEE-HEE! WHEE!
FOOSA, YOUR MAJESTY!
HAVE YOU GONE *CRAZY?!?!*
FAINT!
FOOSA RACING IS A *LEGITIMATE SPORT*, YOUR HIGHNESS, AND A VERY *DANGEROUS ONE*. I'M TOLD THAT *PRINCE AUGUSTINE* IS AN *EXPERT* AT IT!

SHORTLY...
YOU'VE NEVER RIDDEN A FOOSA IN YOUR LIFE, OLD CHAP! GIVE UP NOW AND SAVE YOURSELF FROM FURTHER EMBARRASSMENT!
PLEASE...I AM TRYING TO CONCENTRATE! NOW, WHICH END IS THIS THING'S FACE?
GRRRR
FOUND IT!

I'VE WON THREE CHALLENGES TO YOUR ZERO, AND THIS IS THE LAST BOUT. YOU CAN'T POSSIBLY CATCH UP NOW!
HAH, THE JOKE'S ON YOU! YOU WRONGLY ASSUME I CAN COUNT UP TO THREE!
...OR ZERO!

RUN FOR YOUR LIFE!
AND THEY'RE OFF!
YAAAAAAAAAAAA
I HAVE GOT TO START PAYING MORE ATTENTION!

PRINCE AUGUSTINE STREAKS AHEAD, TAKING THE FIRST BEND WITH REMARKABLE PROWESS--
--WHILE KING JULIEN IS LOSING GROUND WITH EVERY STEP! I'VE NEVER SEEN SUCH A PITIFUL DISPLAY OF FOOSA RIDING!
AAAAAAAHHHHHH!

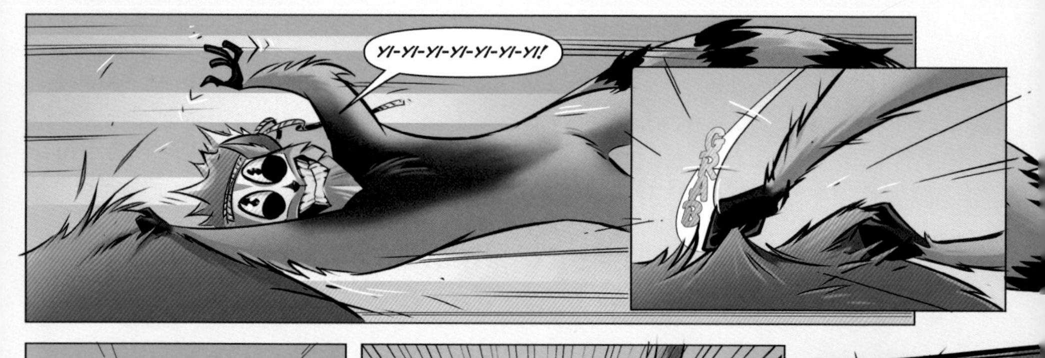
YI-YI-YI-YI-YI-YI-YI-YI!
GRAB

PHEW!
POINK
?
WAIT, RACE FANS, WHAT'S THIS?
KING JULIEN IS MAKING A SUDDEN BREAK FOR FIRST PLACE!
YOOOWWW
GIVE ME BACK MY CROWN, YOU STUPID HAIR BALL!

WHAT--?!
CAN... ALMOST...REACH IT...
...ALMOST...
FASTER, MY VALIANT STEED! FASTER!
GOT YOU!
HUH?
GRRRR!
WHA--? I WON?!!
AND IN FIRST PLACE, KING JULIEN RIDES TO VICTORY--
--WITH PRINCE AUGUSTINE COMING IN DEAD LAST!
LOOK, EVERYBODY-- I WON! I AM THE WINNER!
YES!
FINAL SCORE: PRINCE AUGUSTINE - 3 KING JULIEN - 1
WINNER: PRINCE AUGUSTINE

I AM THE BEST!
BEAT THE REST!
YES, YES, YOU KNOW IT!
THIS IS RIDICULOUS! IT WASN'T A FAIR RACE!!!
ANYONE CAN SEE THAT THIS...THIS... NINCOMPOOP JUST GOT A LUCKY BREAK!
NINCOMPOOP?!
THE WHOLE RACE WAS A...A MOCKERY! A...SHAMBLES! YES, THAT'S IT--A SHAMBLES!
I DEMAND ANOTHER RACE!
NOW, PRINCE AUGUSTINE, WE SHOULD REALLY POINT OUT--
--THAT YOU WON THE OVERALL CONTEST!
IT'S NOT FAIR, I TELL YOU!!!

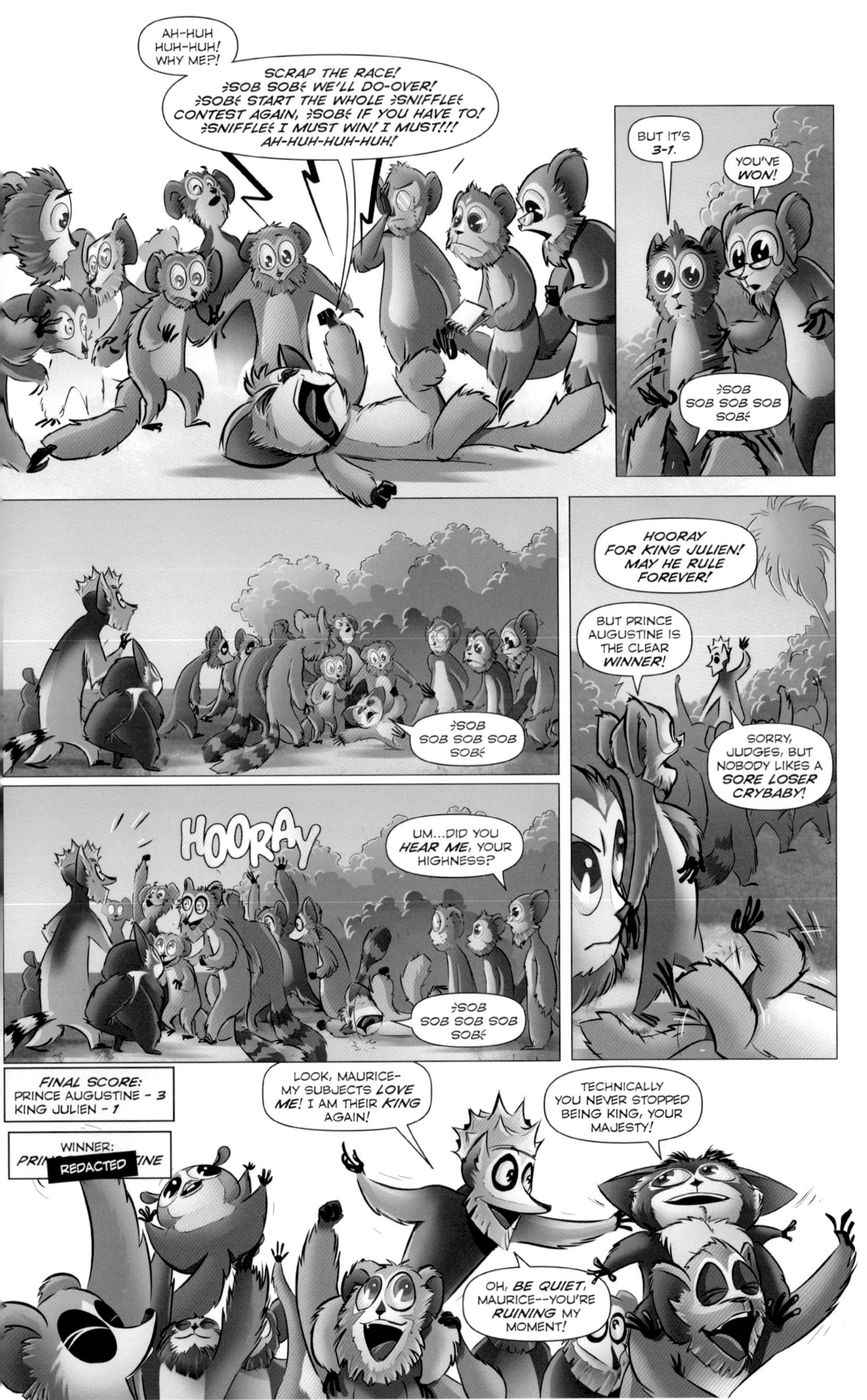

AH-HUH HUH-HUH! WHY ME?!
SCRAP THE RACE! ≯SOB SOB≮ WE'LL DO-OVER! ≯SOB≮ START THE WHOLE ≯SNIFFLE≮ CONTEST AGAIN, ≯SOB≮ IF YOU HAVE TO! ≯SNIFFLE≮ I MUST WIN! I MUST!!! AH-HUH-HUH-HUH!
BUT IT'S 3-1.
YOU'VE WON!
≯SOB SOB SOB SOB SOB≮
≯SOB SOB SOB SOB SOB≮
HOORAY FOR KING JULIEN! MAY HE RULE FOREVER!
BUT PRINCE AUGUSTINE IS THE CLEAR WINNER!
SORRY, JUDGES, BUT NOBODY LIKES A SORE LOSER CRYBABY!
HOORAY
UM...DID YOU HEAR ME, YOUR HIGHNESS?
≯SOB SOB SOB SOB SOB≮
FINAL SCORE: PRINCE AUGUSTINE - 3 KING JULIEN - 1
WINNER: PRIN REDACTED INE
LOOK, MAURICE- MY SUBJECTS LOVE ME! I AM THEIR KING AGAIN!
TECHNICALLY YOU NEVER STOPPED BEING KING, YOUR MAJESTY!
OH, BE QUIET, MAURICE--YOU'RE RUINING MY MOMENT!

ALL HAIL KING JULIEN!

YES, YES, ALL HAIL *ME!*

KING OF THE LEMURS!

MAURICE, MORT-- COME UP HERE, YOU SCALLYWAGS!

YOU TWO ***STOOD BY ME*** THROUGHOUT THIS WHOLE ***LUDICROUS AFFAIR***.

NOW, I NEED YOU TO STAND VERY STILL--
--I'VE NOT DONE THIS BEFORE!
YIKES!
FAINT!
UM, IF IT'S ALL THE SAME TO YOU, YOUR MAGNIFICENCE, I'D RATHER STAY ONE OF THE LOWLY COMMON FOLK.
OH, BUT, MAURICE-- YOU'D MAKE SUCH A GOOD KNIGHT! YOU COULD GO ON QUESTS!
LET ME THROUGH!
I PROMISE IT WON'T HURT! COME BACK!
A KNIGHT HAS TO BE BRAVE, MAURICE!
COME BACK!!!
THE END

DreamWorks

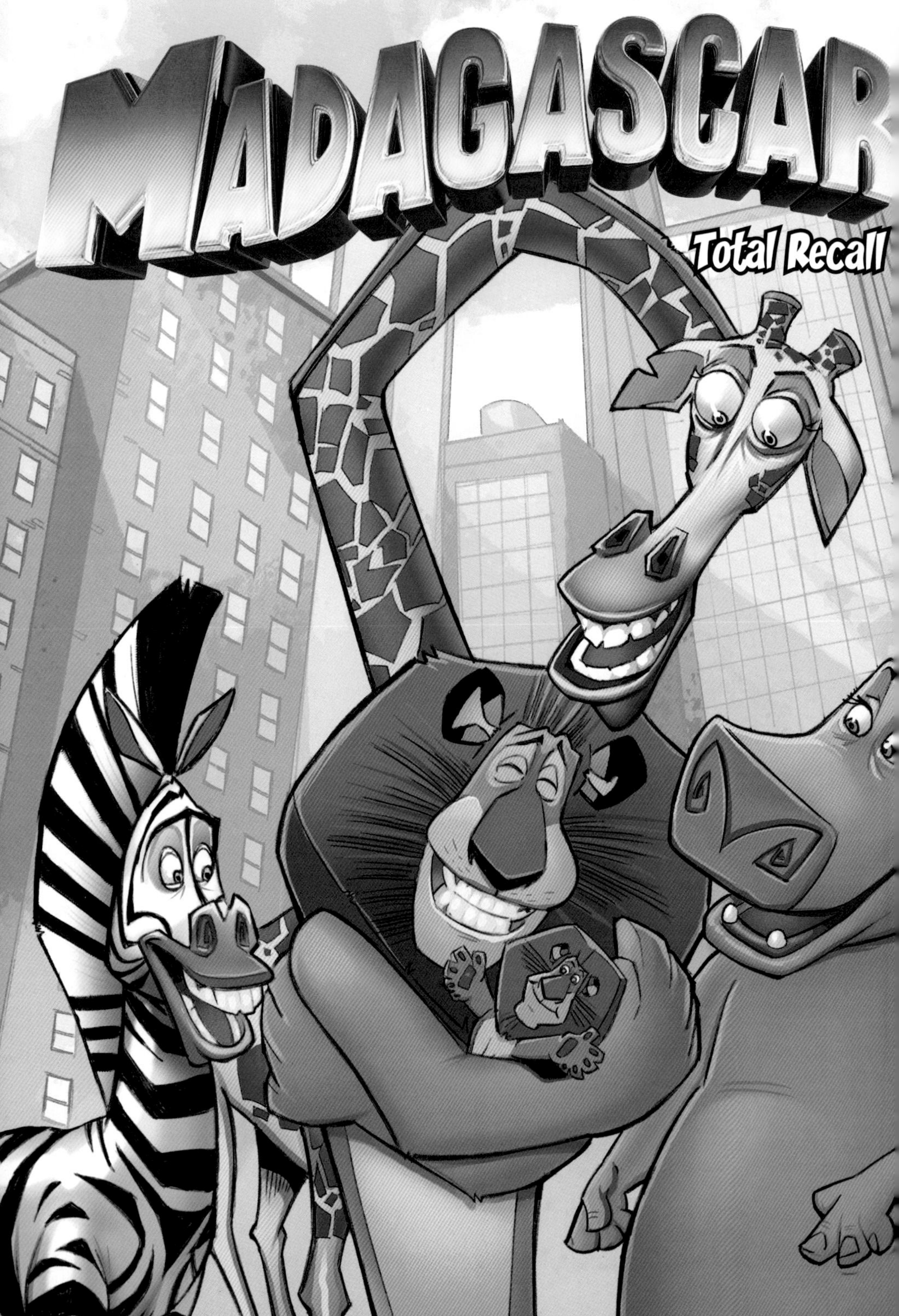

PRESENTING...
...ALEX THE LION!
ROAAAARR
HOORAY
CLAP
CLAP
CLAP

Zoo Gifty
MELMAN, MARTY--WOULD YOU LOOK AT THIS CROWD?
I KNOW, GLORIA! I'VE NEVER SEEN SO MANY PEOPLE IN ONE PLACE! I THINK I MAY HAVE CAUGHT SOMETHING!
MELMAN, GLORIA--SHHH. THEY'RE ABOUT TO MAKE--

"--THE BIG ANNOUNCEMENT!"
WE HERE AT THE CENTRAL PARK ZOO ARE PROUD TO REVEAL OUR NEW OFFICIAL FAN CLUB!
STARTING TODAY, ALL YOU SPECIAL BOYS AND GIRLS WHO LOVE ANIMALS SO MUCH--
ALEX №1

--CAN BE A PART OF OUR EXCITING FAMILY!
WHEN YOU JOIN, YOU'LL GET ALL THIS--A SUPER POSTER, FANTASTIC FACT FILES, A BUTTON, A GREAT PEN, DECALS...

...AND YOUR VERY OWN--
--ROARING ALEX!

ROAAARR
squeeze
ROAAAARR
CLAP
CLAP
CLAP

NO WONDER ALEX COULDN'T SLEEP LAST NIGHT--WHO WOULDN'T WANT TO BE THE MASCOT OF THE ZOO'S FAN CLUB?
HE'S EARNED THIS! HE SHOULD BE *PROUD!*
tick
CLAP
CLAP
CLAP
WELL, YOU KNOW WHAT THEY SAY--*A LION'S NOTHING WITHOUT HIS PRIDE!*

I WANT ONE!
DADDY? CAN I HAVE A LITTLE ALEX?
GIMME GIMME!
ROAR!

THEY'RE *SO CUTE...*
...I THINK I'M GOING TO *CRY!* *SNIFF*
TOUGHEN UP, SOLDIER, THERE'S NO SPACE FOR *CRY-BABIES* IN THIS OUTFIT!

WHA--? WHO ARE YOU AGAIN?
THE BOYS AND JUST BREEZED OVER ROM THE *COOL SIDE* OF THE ZOO!
IT'S SO CROWDED, I CAN'T SEE A--

--THING!
OOPS!
PENGUIN OVERBOARD! *WAAA!*
BUMP
INTEGRITY HAS BEEN *COMPROMISED.* REPEAT--WE HAVE BEEN *COMPROMISED!*

YOU KNOW, GUYS, I'VE NEVER SEEN ALEX LOOK *SO HAPPY!*
YEAH!

SHORTLY...
DIDJA SEE, GUYS? WHEN I DID THIS, AND THEN--
ROAAARR
--ISN'T IT AWESOME?
WELLLLL, I WOULDN'T GO SO FAR AS TO SAY AWESOME...
IGNORE MELMAN! IT'S A REAL ACHIEVEMENT, ALEX. YOU'RE--
I KNOW! THOSE KIDS--THEY LOVE ME!
ME! ALEX THE LION! EVERY FAN CLUB MEMBER GETS A LITTLE ME! HOW COOL IS THAT?
I TELL YOU GUYS, I'M MORE POPULAR THAN--
--THE BEETLES!
INSECT HOUSE
TO BE FAIR, ALEX, THE ZOO'S INSECT HOUSE DOESN'T ATTRACT THAT MANY VISITORS!
WE'RE PLEASED FOR YOU, ALEX. ALL OF US. RIGHT, GUYS?
RIGHT!

LATER...
PSSST! DOWN HERE, MARTY!
OKAY.
MAN, I WAS NOT BUILT FOR ROCK CLIMBING!

IN THERE!
WHOAAAAA-OH-OH-OH!

MAN-O-MAN, YOU'D THINK THEY WERE TRYING TO KEEP US ANIMALS AWAY FROM HERE!
PTUI!!

IT'S SO BEAUTIFUL!

UM... WHAT ARE WE LOOKING AT?

FAN CLUB KITS BEING BOXED UP! HUNDREDS OF LITTLE ALEXES BRAVING THE OUT-SIDE WORLD TO BRING JOY TO ALL THOSE KIDS!
IT'S HUMBLING, ISN'T IT?
YOU KNOW, ALEX, HUMBLE ISN'T A WORD THAT HAS EVER CROSSED MY MIND WHEN THINKING ABOUT YOU!

THAT NIGHT--
ALEX
Nº 1
--ALEX DREAMS OF HOW POPULAR HE IS--
ROHAARR
PRESENTING THE INCREDIBLE... ALEX THE LION!
ALEX
--AND HOW POPULAR HE COULD BE!
HE'S SO "THIS SEASON!"
HE'S EVERY SEASON!

THE KING OF THE JUNGLE HAS ENTERED THE BUILDING!
THANK YOU, THANK YOU VERY MUCH!
...WOULD LIKE TO WELCOME THE NEW PRESIDENT OF THE UNITED STATES OF AMERICA--
--ALEX THE LION!
ALEX...? HEY, ALEX--

--WAKE UP!
HUH? MARTY?
WHAT IS IT? I WAS HAVING THE MOST WONDERFUL DREAM!
YOU'D BETTER PREPARE YOURSELF-- THERE'S BEEN SOME BAD NEWS, BUDDY.
WHAT? IT'S NOT MELMAN...?
GLORIA...?
IS IT...THE BEETLES? DID THE BEETLES SPLIT UP? DON'T TELL ME THAT THE BEETLES HAVE SPLIT UP!
NO, IT'S WORSE. THIS IS IN TODAY'S NEWSPAPER.
ZOO FAN CLUB TOYS TO BE RECALLED!
THE CENTRAL PARK ZOO IS REELING TODAY AFTER TRAGEDY STRUCK ITS NEWLY-FORMED FAN CLUB.
CLUB OFFICIALS DISCOVERED LATE YESTERDAY EVENING THAT A FAULTY BATCH OF TOYS REPRESENTING ITS MASCOT, ALEX THE LION, WAS ACCIDENTALLY SHIPPED TO EAGERLY WAITING FANS.
INSTEAD OF THE LION'S USUAL ROAR, THE CUDDLY ALEX TOYS MAKE ANOTHER NOISE ASSOCIATED WITH NEW YORK CITY-- A NOISE POPULARLY KNOWN AS THE "BRONX CHEER."
WHAT'S A BRONX CHEER?
PFFFTT!
OH NO!

OH, MAN.
HE IS TAKING THIS REALLY BAD.
MARTY SHOULD TALK TO HIM. HE'S ALEX'S BEST FRIEND.
PFFFTT!
PFFFTT!
PFFFTT!

WILL YOU GUYS QUIT IT?
PFFFTT! OOPS, SORRY, GLORIA!

HEY, BUDDY. WHATCHA DOING?
LETTING EVERYONE DOWN.

AW, C'MON. IT'S NOT SO BAD.
ALL THOSE FANS WERE RELYING ON ME TO BE THERE FOR THEM, MARTY. WELL, ME IN THE FORM OF "LI'L ALEX" HERE.

I'VE LET THEM ALL DOWN.
ROAAARR

I HEAR YA, BUDDY. IT'S TOUGH BEING THE IDOL OF MILLIONS. IT'S SURE NOT A RESPONSIBILITY I'D WANT. BUT YOU, YOU PLAY IT COOL. YOU'RE ALWAYS--

--ALEX! THE! LION!
ROAR!

SEE? I CAN'T PULL THIS OFF-- I JUST LOOK LIKE AN IDIOT!
AND NEITHER COULD MELMAN OR GLORIA OR SKIPPER OR ANY OF THE OTHERS.

BUT YOU, MAN--YOU'RE THE KING OF THE JUNGLE!
A LITTLE SETBACK LIKE THIS TOY ALEX THING-- THAT'S NOTHING TO THE KING. THE KING TAKES IT IN STRIDE, SHRUGS IT OFF. AND MOVES ON.

YOU'RE RIGHT, MARTY! I CAN FIX THIS.
THAT'S THE SPIRIT!

FIRST, I'LL NEED THE NAME AND ADDRESS OF EVERY FAN CLUB MEMBER WHO'S RECEIVED A BROKEN ALEX TOY.
HUH? WELL...

THEN, I'LL SNEAK INTO THEIR HOUSES AND STEAL THE TOYS BACK!
OH, LIKE SANTA CLAUS! ONLY IN REVERSE!
EXACTLY!

AND I'LL REPLACE THE OLD TOYS WITH COOL NEW TOYS! ONES THAT ROAR.
ROAAARR
YEAH!

WHAT DO YOU SAY, MARTY? ARE YOU WITH ME?
JUST TRY AN' STOP ME!

NOW, CAN I QUIT POSING LIKE THIS? IT'S REALLY STARTING TO HURT!

THAT EVENING...

tap
tap
tap
tap

GRRSHN
GRRSHN

WHRRR
WHRRR

click

DID YOU GET IT?

DID WE GET IT? HAH! WHAT DO YOU TAKE US FOR, HIPPIE-HAIR-- ROOKIES?

RICO, SHOW HIM!
AND IT HAS THE ADDRESS FOR EVERY FAN CLUB MEMBER?
EVERY ONE!

ACCORDING TO PHIL, THE FAN CLUB ADDRESSES HAVE BEEN CROSS-REFERENCED WITH THE BATCH NUMBERS FOR THE FAULTY TOYS! AND THEY'RE ALL IN NEW YORK, OR CLOSE BY!
HEAR THAT, ALEX? TRACKING DOWN THE DISAPPOINTED FANS WILL BE EASY!
AND I'VE SECURED US SOME WORKING REPLACEMENTS FROM THE GIFT SHOP STORAGE ROOM, JUST LIKE YOU ASKED--TESTED THEM ALL MYSELF!
WAS IT DIFFICULT?
ROAAARR
ROAAARR
ROAAARR
"EASY PEASY!"
FIRST STOP, NEW JERSEY!
ROAD TRIP!

NEW JERSEY...
THIS IS THE ADDRESS, MARTY.
DON'T GIVE ME THAT LOOK, ALEX-- THIS WAS YOUR IDEA!
ZZZ
OKAY, OKAY. HAND ME THAT LITTLE ALEX.
ROAAARR
HUH? WHUZZAT...? ZZZZZZZZZZZ
GOT IT!
YOU'RE SURE IT'S THE RIGHT ONE?
PFFTT!
OH YEAH!

THE EMPIRE STATE BUILDING...
WHY AM I DOING THIS AGAIN??
FOR WIDER DISTRIBUTION!
PRINCETON, NEW JERSEY...
THIS TAKES A DEGREE... OF FINESSE!
BROADWAY...
MOMMY? THAT CAT LOOKS WEIRD!
HE'S RIGHT! WHY DIDN'T ALEX TAKE THIS ASSIGNMENT?
ROCKEFELLER CENTER...
KEEP THE LINE MOVING!
CHINATOWN...
WHAT ARE WE DOING HERE?
FORGET IT, ALEX; IT'S CHINATOWN!
THE EMPIRE STATE BUILDIN
(AGAIN)...
COME NOW, PHIL, MUST YOU BE SO CLICHÉ?
WHEEEEEEE!

THE HOLLAND TUNNEL...
STEP ON THE GAS, GLORIA!
I *CAN'T*-- THIS THING'S *ELECTRIC!*
JUST GET US *CLOSE!*

AND... *DEPLOY!*
TIGHT FORMATION, BOYS! *GO! GO!*
OW! OW! OW! OH, WAIT-THAT'S REALLY WORKING THE KNOTS OUT OF MY--

OW! NO, IT'S *NOT!*
I'VE GOT IT!
PFFTT!
AND-- *SWITCH!*

CHANGE LANES! CHANGE LANES!
BEEP BEEP

YIIIII!
fwip fwip
CLONK

I'VE GOT YOU! *JUMP!*
WHOA!

THE TRIP TAKES THE GANG ALL OVER...

--SOMEWHERE!

WESTCHESTER...

I HAVE THE BROKEN TOY, MARTY! NOW, HURRY--
--HAND ME THAT REPLACEMENT!
WE'RE ALL OUT OF REPLACEMENTS! WE'VE USED THE LAST LI'L ALEX, PAL!
WHU...? IS SOMEONE...?

THE KID'S WAKING UP! WHAT DO I DO?
I DON'T KNOW! IMPROVISE!

YAWN!

I LOVE YOU, ALEX.
ROAAARR
Poke

SMOOTH WORK, BUDDY!
zzzz

PSSST! WHAT'S KEEPING YOU TWO?
WE'VE RUN OUT OF L'IL ALEX TOYS!
HERE! THIS IS THE LAST BAG! NOW, HURRY IT UP, OKAY?
BUT THERE ARE NO LIONS IN HERE! JUST...ZEBRAS AND...HIPPOS AND ...GIRAFFES.
WHAT ARE WE GONNA DO?
YOU KNOW SOMETHING, MARTY? I THINK ANY KID WOULD BE PROUD TO HAVE A ZEBRA OR A HIPPO OR A GIRAFFE JUST AS MUCH--
--AS A LION.
GREAT! THEN, LET'S GET ON WITH IT--
"--WE STILL HAVE TEN MORE HOUSES TO VISIT!"

THE NEXT MORNING...
LOOK!
COOOOOOOL!

WHERE DID YOU GET THAT, SWEETIE?
THE FAIRIES LEFT IT FOR ME!

I THOUGHT WE GOT JACK A LION?
YEAH, ME TOO! I GUESS WE DIDN'T LOOK PROPERLY!

ROAAARR
ROAAARR
ROAAARR

PRESENTING...

...ALEX...

...THE LION!

ROAAARR

CENTRAL PARK ZOO...
YOU DID IT, AL-EX!

YOU REPLACED EVERY FAULTY TOY!
YEAH, I GUESS I *DID!*

NO--
--*WE* DID IT.

I *COULDN'T* HAVE DONE ANY-THING WITHOUT *ALL* OF YOU.
THANKS, ALEX.

Zoo Gifty
I MEAN IT! I MAY BE THE STAR OF THE ZOO, BUT YOU GUYS HAVE ALWAYS BEEN JUST AS MUCH A PART OF THE SHOW.

AND, YOU KNOW, I WOULDN'T BE HALF THE STAR I AM WITHOUT SUCH GREAT FRIENDS BEHIND ME.
COME ON, BRING IT IN! YOU KNOW YOU WANT TO.

YEAH!

HEY, DOES ANYONE KNOW WHAT HAPPENED TO ALL THOSE FAULTY ALEX TOYS WE SNATCHED?
SKIPPER SAID THAT HE'D DEAL WITH THEM.

SEWHERE...
CHARGE!
ANY IDEA WHERE THEY'LL END UP, SKIPPER?
NOT OUR PROBLEM, PRIVATE!
SPLASH

EPILOGUE.

THE EN